SPIDER SANDWICHES

Claire Freedman   illustrated by Sue Hendra
and Paul Linnet

BLOOMSBURY
NEW YORK   LONDON   NEW DELHI   SYDNEY

Come eat with Max.
He has a MONSTER appetite!

He eats such yucky, mucky food,
his mealtimes are a fright.

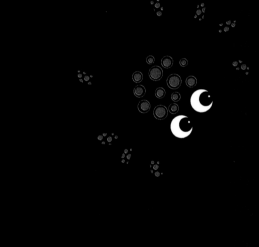

He LOVES to glug slug milkshakes,
through a stinky hosepipe straw.

And as for beetle cookies—
he can ALWAYS munch one more!

For breakfast every morning,
he chews toenail scrambled eggs.

Then guzzles down a smoothie,
made from crushed grasshopper legs!

He buys snacks on the Internet,
from as far away as space...

spiky space ants, moon-goo globs,
are all stuffed in his face!

By lunchtime Max is STARVING.
"Scrumptious lice rice—I can't wait!"

He slurps it SUPER fast before
the lice crawl off his plate!

He bought the *Monsters' Cookbook*,
for some recipe ideas.

The best was slimed-eel noodles,
served with hairy fried bats' ears!

From pickled worms to squashed fly jam,
Max beams, "Hooray! Yes, please!"

He spreads them on his crackers —POOH—
with smelly fish-eye cheese.

"So delicious!" gurgles Max,
with a massive goo-filled grin...

cold, crunchy cockroach chowder,
drip-dribbling down his chin.

tadpole ice cream, snail trail sauce,
things that squirm and slurp...

they ALL mix in his tummy—
look out! Here comes a BURP!

Rat's tail pizza, blue mold chips,
bug burgers are a treat.

But when it comes to mealtime,
there's ONE thing he will ALWAYS eat...

Squiggly spider sandwiches!
He scarfs them down so fast.

He eats their heads and sticky webs,
but saves their legs for last!

Max will eat up anything
that oozes gunk and gloop.

But even MONSTERS gasp, "No, thanks!"
when faced with...

GREEN
SPROUT
SOUP!

To Michael, who's not afraid of spiders x
—CF

For lovely Steve who adores food but, unlike Max,
has impeccable table manners —SH

First published in Great Britain in October 2013 by Bloomsbury Publishing Plc
Published in the United States of America in July 2014 by Bloomsbury Children's Books
www.bloomsbury.com

Bloomsbury is a registered trademark of Bloomsbury Publishing Plc

For information about permission to reproduce selections from this book, write to Permissions, Bloomsbury Children's Books, 1385 Broadway, New York, New York 10018
Bloomsbury books may be purchased for business or promotional use. For information on bulk purchases please contact Macmillan Corporate and Premium Sales Department at specialmarkets@macmillan.com

Library of Congress Cataloging-in-Publication Data
Freedman, Claire.
Spider sandwiches / by Claire Freedman ; illustrated by Sue Hendra.
pages   cm
Summary: Monster Max will feast on anything crawly, creepy, hairy, and sticky, but his favorite snack is squirmy spider sandwiches.
ISBN 978-1-61963-364-3 (hardcover) • ISBN 978-1-61963-365-0 (reinforced)
[1. Stories in rhyme. 2. Food habits—Fiction. 3. Monsters—Fiction. 4. Humorous stories.] I. Hendra, Sue, illustrator. II. Title.
PZ8.3.F885Sp 2014   [E]—dc23   2013034319

Art created with Adobe Photoshop • Typeset in Neucha • Book design by Zoe Waring

Printed in China by C&C Offset Printing Co., Ltd., Shenzhen, Guangdong
2 4 4 8 10 9 7 5 3 1 (hardcover)
2 4 6 8 10 9 7 5 3 1 (reinforced)

All papers used by Bloomsbury Publishing, Inc. are natural, recyclable products made from wood grown in well-managed forests.
The manufacturing processes conform to the environmental regulations of the country of origin.